With love, to Lyra Arabella

ISBN: 978-1-7377213-0-7

Publisher Mindful Pixel LLC

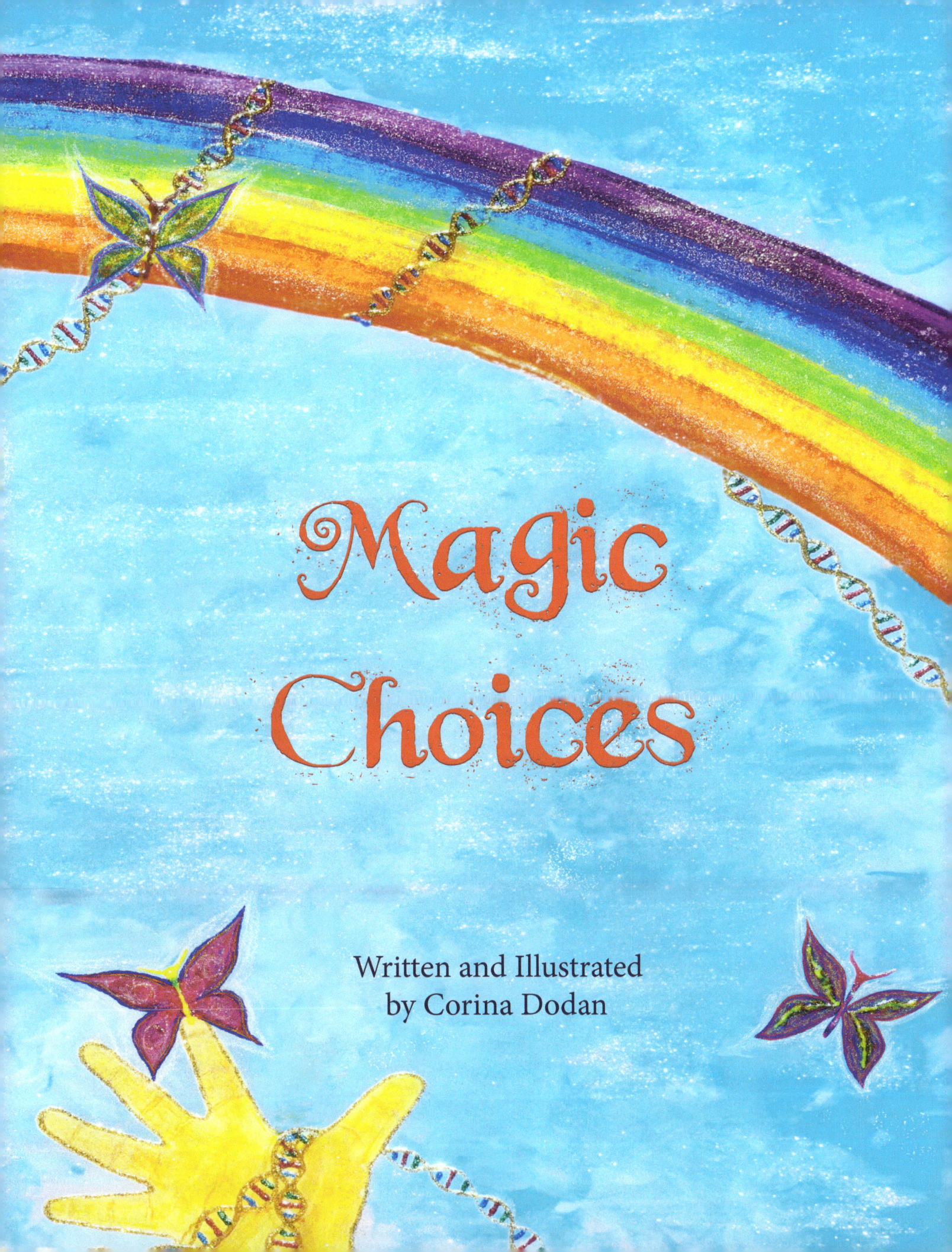

Magic
Choices

Written and Illustrated
by Corina Dodan

"Mommy, what is magic?" Lyra asked curiously.
"All life is magic. You are magic too!"
Mommy said smiling.

"As you grow, a magic garden also grows in your mind and the plants will start from magic, sparkly seeds." Mommy said.

"Where can we buy
sparkly seeds?
I love sparkles!"
Lyra exclaimed.

"They are free for everyone.
We live in an infinite ocean of
magic seeds. They are invisible,
like our thoughts." Mommy said.

"What do you mean?
What are they?" Lyra asked.

"I'm the seed of joy!
Pick me, pick me!"

"I'm the seed of love! Pick me too!"

"I'm the seed of creativity.
I want to grow and make beautiful things."

"I'm the seed of genius mind!
Pick me!"

"I'm the seed of wealth. Pick me!"

"I'm the seed of health. Pick me,
I will help you grow into all of your dreams!"

More magic seeds, like strength, kindness,
generosity, persistence... called to be picked!

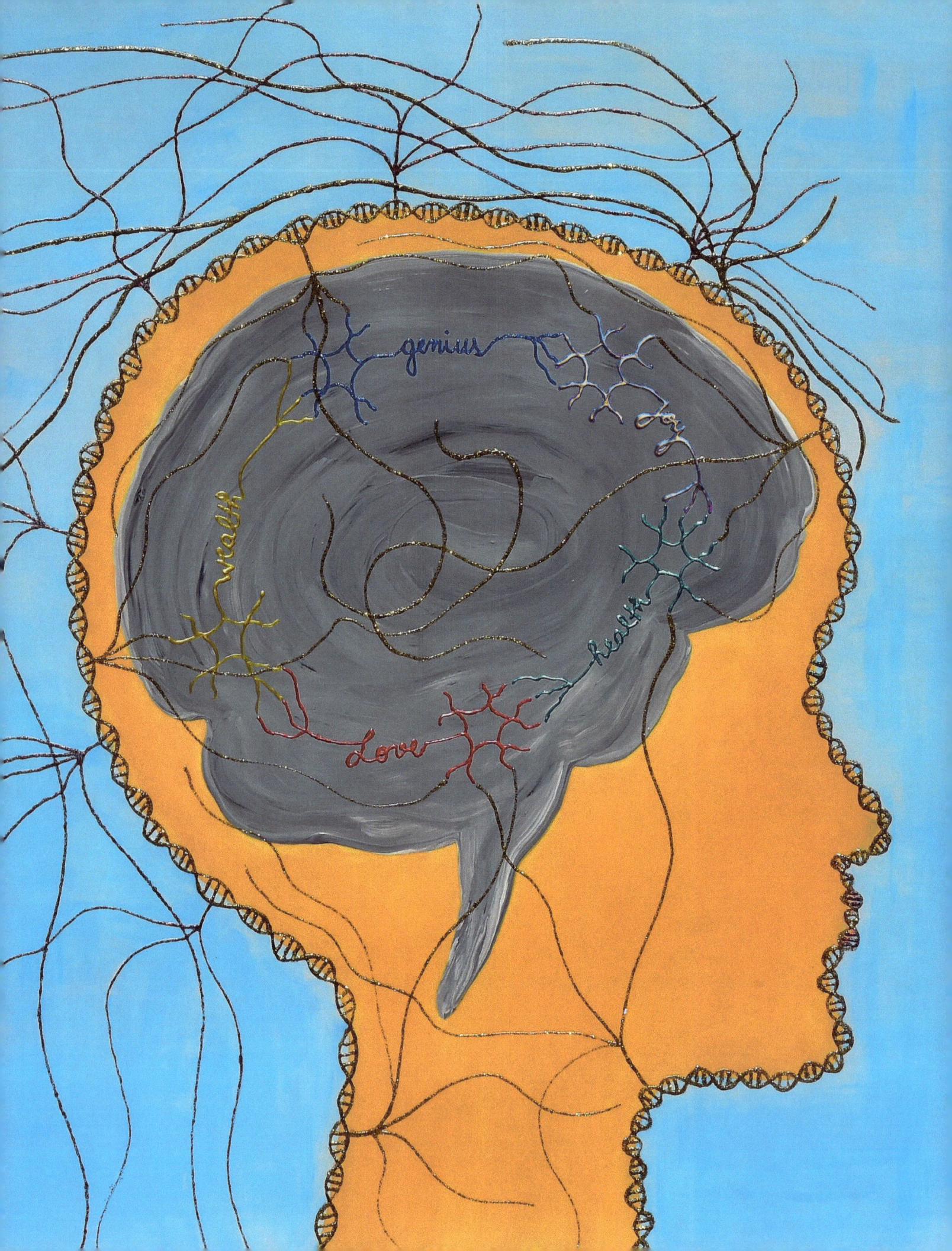

"It's fun to care for
your mind.

If a seed is in your mind,
and you don't like it,
you can give it up.

Move your mind to the
seeds you want to grow."
Mommy said.

"Hold the seeds in your mind and
you will grow to be one with your magic choices."
Mommy said.

"Mommy, how do these seeds
grow in my mind?
What do I do?" Lyra asked.

"I'm glad you asked!
Questions are the beginning
of every adventure." Mommy said.

"When you think about love, for example,
your mind will come up with loving ideas.
You'll start to see love everywhere."
Mommy said.

"You can keep a journal
where you write about your day
and how your seeds are growing."
Mommy said.

"Another way
to care for your seeds
is to have a vision board
where you can draw
your choices."
Mommy said.

"If something bothers you,
stop and check your magic garden.

You get to choose
how you want to feel,
what you want to be,
or what you want to explore.

It's okay to change your mind
and that's magic too."
Mommy said.

"What else can I do
in my magic garden?"
Lyra asked.

"So much more,
and you'll learn it all.
For now,
ask questions,
write
and draw."
Mommy said.

What would you like to plant in
your magic mind?

What would you like
to be, to do, and to have?

About the Author

I am a mother, a traveler, and a lover of knowledge. From sciences
to arts, music and spirituality, I research and study everything my
mind seeks to understand.

Reading to my daughter I fell in love with children's books.
After the many classes I took about mind programming,
I was aware of the impact of words and images on her mind.

I wanted to read to her more mindful books
and at times they were hard to find.
That made me dive into writing and illustrating books.

I believe great children's books leave kids empowered to build
confidence and self-esteem so they can grow
to be strong individuals.

I create books to inspire children to dream
of mindful possibilities because life is knitted
in our dreams with the threads of thoughts and beliefs.

Thank you for taking the time to read my books to children!

Acknowledgments

I'm grateful to my parents for their
immeasurable efforts to raise me and my brothers
to have choices in life.

I'm grateful to my daughter for her presence
and for her infinite love.

I'm grateful to the teachers who planted
countless sparkly seeds in my mind.

Other Magic Books coming up:

Magic Luggage

Magic Dark

MAGIC QUESTIONS

Magic chocolate

Magic thoughts

Magic words

Magic invisibility

Magic nutrients

And so many more...

www.ingramcontent.com/pod-product-compliance
Lightning Source LLC
Chambersburg PA
CBHW041720240626
47171CB00002B/18